Happy Like Soccer

Maribeth Boelts
illustrated by Lauren Castillo

CANDLEWICK PRESS

NOTHING MAKES ME HAPPY LIKE SOCCER—
picked for this new team,
with these shiny girls.

My shoes have flames and my ball spins
on this spread-out sea of grass with no weeds,
fields with no holes, and real goals,
not two garbage cans shoved together
like in the lot by my apartment,
where soccer means
any kid who shows up can play.

But nothing makes me sad like soccer, too,
because the restaurant where my auntie works
is busy on Saturdays and she can't take time off
for something like a soccer game.

Early every game day,
my auntie looks me over good—brushes my hair,
rubs my legs with lotion.
She says, "Have fun and play hard, Sierra."
I smile, but when she hugs me good-bye,
I know she can feel me low around the edges.

Then my ride comes,
filled with laughing girls
who know the jokes I don't.
We weave past the empty lot
and through my neighborhood
and outside the city,
where the buses don't run.

When the game starts,
I do play hard and I do have fun,
but my eyes have their own mind,
spying the sidelines, where families sit on blankets
and wave from foldout chairs.

They cheer for me by the number on my uniform,
not knowing my name.
Every girl has someone there but me.

Coach Marco high-fives me
and tells me he is glad I am on the team.
When he asks me if there's anything I need,
I bite my lip without meaning to
and tell him no.

After the game,
we ride back home, into the city,
through my neighborhood,
past the empty lot,
and right to the restaurant,
where my auntie brings me chicken and noodles.
On her break, we talk about the game
and what-all happened as best as I remember.

Then on Friday, my auntie tells me that her boss has heard me talking. He asked her if she would like to trade her shift on Saturday for one on Sunday so she could come to my last game.
"What did you tell him?" I ask.
My auntie laughs. "I said, 'Yes, of course I would.'"
Then we dance a made-up dance in the kitchen and bake a cherry cake, the way we always do when there's celebrating going on.

That night, I am so excited that I dream about soccer.
In my dream, I am running so fast that I lift off the ground a little bit.
Even my ball is in the air.

"Flying dreams mean you're feeling fine," my auntie says in the morning,
and she is right.

My auntie and I travel to the game together,
riding on one bus past the empty lot,
then another through the city,
then walking the rest of the way to the fields.

But when my game is ready to start,
I feel it.
Fat raindrops plopping.
Then thunder starts its show,
and in the distance, lightning.

Coach Marco gathers us up quick and says the game is canceled
but will be rescheduled.
I swallow,
sure that the rescheduled last game will be on a Saturday,
sure it will be outside the city,
sure my auntie's boss won't do two favors right in a row.

Coach Marco gives me and my auntie a ride back home.
In the car, my auntie sits by close, her hand warm, covering my knee.

At home, we play cards and eat cherry cake
and look at old pictures.
My auntie pulls out the funny ones to make me feel better,
and I would, except I'm thinking hard.

When she tucks me in, I'm still thinking . . .

about the empty lot by my apartment
and my auntie's day off being Monday,
and I wonder if maybe this time,
for this last game,
I can answer Coach Marco's question about if there's anything
I'm needing with something true.

My auntie is asleep, so I tiptoe to the kitchen.

My heart is thumping the way it does when
my teacher calls on me even though I haven't raised my hand.
I dial the first part of Coach Marco's phone number and hang up, shaky.
I wait and try again.
Coach Marco answers.

I take a breath and tell him I'm sorry for it being late, and
then I say my idea fast and all run-on, that maybe the game
could be on a Monday,
and maybe it could be at the lot by my apartment,
and then maybe my auntie could come?

Coach Marco is quiet, listening.
Then he says he'll make some calls.
"I can't promise, Sierra," he says. "But I'll let you know."

It is a long time until morning.
City sounds are all around,
mixed with
my auntie's steady breathing,
and my own self noisy
with what I want to happen.

Later, Coach Marco shows up at the lot
to see for himself
and tells me that my idea was a good one.
"This will work for everyone," he says, smiling.

I run home, skipping the stairs two at a time.
My words spill the story,
and my auntie tips my chin up
and looks at me, both amazed and proud.

"You did that for me?" she says.
I nod, and she pulls me close.
"For me, too," I say.

At the last game, there are families on blankets,
and people waving from foldout chairs.

There are faces from my neighborhood, too,
on bikes, stopping by, with all the others.

And I hear my name because they know *me*,
not just my number.
And above the rest, I hear
my auntie's strong voice cheering me on.

And I run so fast that this time, I know for real that I am flying.

To Heidi and Andy for being inspiring examples of
what it means to cheer from the sidelines
M. B.

For the DeLanty family
L. C.

Text copyright © 2012 by Maribeth Boelts
Illustrations copyright © 2012 by Lauren Castillo

First paperback edition 2014

Library of Congress Cataloging-in-Publication Data is available.

Library of Congress Catalog Card Number 2011018624

ISBN 978-0-7636-4616-5 (hardcover)
ISBN 978-0-7636-7049-8 (paperback)

15 16 17 18 SWT 10 9 8 7 6 5 4

Printed in Dongguan, Guangdong, China

This book was typeset in ITC Leawood.
The illustrations were done in ink and watercolor with acetone transfer.

Candlewick Press
99 Dover Street
Somerville, Massachusetts 02144

visit us at www.candlewick.com